The Jur g

Story by Wendy Macdonald
Illustrations by Pat Reynolds

PM Chapter Books
part of the Rigby PM Collection

U.S. edition © 2001 Rigby
a division of Reed Elsevier Inc.
1000 Hart Road
Barrington, IL 60010-2627
www.rigby.com

Text © Nelson Thomson Learning 2000
Illustrations © Nelson Thomson Learning 2000
Originally published in Australia by Nelson Thomson Learning

06 05 04 03 02 01
10 9 8 7 6 5 4 3 2

The Junkyard Dog
ISBN 0 7635 7450 3

Printed in China by Midas Printing (Asia) Ltd.

Contents

Chapter 1

Prince

The first time I saw Prince, I was walking home from swimming.

I had to walk past a junkyard full of old cars, with a chain-link fence around it. From inside this fence came a growl—a low rumble that said, "Back off!" Then I saw the dog. His lips were drawn back in a snarl.

"Hello," I said timidly. "I'm Rachel. What's your name?"

I moved toward him, but he barked so savagely that I stopped dead. He was thin and his coat looked rough and dull.

"They don't give you much to eat, do they?" I asked him. He growled again. "No," I said. "I thought not."

That night we had T-bone steak for dinner, and after I'd cleared away my plate, I smuggled my bone out of the kitchen.

The next day, on my way to swimming, I pushed it through the fence. The dog snapped it in two with one bite.

"Poor thing," I said. "You must be so hungry."

After that I took him our leftovers every time I went swimming. At first he growled at me, but soon he became quieter and even seemed pleased to see me. He wagged his tail when he saw me coming, and one day I felt brave enough to pat him through a hole in the fence.

"I'm going to call you Prince," I told him, and he licked my hand.

Chapter 2

Stewart Rider

I took up swimming because I have asthma and the doctor said it might help. Every day when school was over, I went to the pool because we were training hard for the swim meet. Our coach, Mr. Shaw, thought we could win the girls' relay, and I really wanted to make the team.

One day as I approached the junkyard, I heard barking and shouting and rattling.

Stewart Rider was kicking the fence, and Prince was flinging himself against it.

"Come on. Let's see you jump. Up, boy!" shouted Stewart. Stewart was about the same age as my older brother, and he was known to be a loser. He worked after school at a local gas station.

"Stop it," I yelled, running up to the fence. "You're making that dog mad!"

"No, I'm not," said Stewart. "Gives him something to do." And he kicked the fence again.

"You're teasing him," I protested. "You're making him vicious."

"He's supposed to be vicious. He's a guard dog isn't he?"

"You're cruel," I shouted. "Leave him alone!"

Stewart looked surprised. "What do you care?" he asked. "It's only a dog."

Chapter 3

Prince Is Missing

The next day after swimming, I set off for home. As I neared the junkyard, I could see that it was empty. I ran to the gates, but they were chained and padlocked.

I was looking in the yard for any sign of Prince, when Stewart came along.

"What happened here?" I asked.

"Last night all the stuff was loaded onto a big trailer, and today," he shrugged, "there's nothing."

"Did you see Prince?" I asked. "You know, that dog you were teasing."

"Nah. I suppose they took him away with the rest of the junk," said Stewart.

But I wasn't so sure. Those people hadn't fed him properly and would think nothing of leaving him behind.

I looked around me. Parts of the junkyard were covered in long grass. But ... something was moving. I took a closer look. There was Prince, tied to an old tree stump. He had no food or water!

"Oh, Prince!" I ran toward him.

"Watch out! That dog's vicious," said Stewart, backing off. "He'll bite you."

"No, he won't," I said. "You're my friend, aren't you boy?"

Prince wagged his tail as I pulled a chunk of last night's roast beef from my pocket. He gobbled it hungrily.

"Come on boy," I said, untying the rope. "I'm taking you home."

When we reached home, Mom said,
"Oh, Rachel, what have you brought back
now?" Prince wasn't the first animal I'd
brought home—we already had two
rabbits and a cat.

"This is Prince," I announced.
"Please can we keep him, Mom? He's a
good watchdog. He'll look after us."

So Prince stayed, and after a few weeks of loving care, he put on weight and his coat became thick and shiny.

Chapter 4

Stewart Starts Training

The time for the swim meet drew nearer. I was in bed every night before nine. In the morning I did exercises, and every afternoon Prince came with me to the pool.

One day, on the way to the pool, we met Stewart Rider. "Hasn't that dog eaten you yet?" he smirked.

"He's my friend," I said proudly. "He watches me while I'm training."

"You sure do spend a lot of time swimming."

"Yeah," I answered, "I like it." Then I
added, "You should come, too." I don't
know why I said that. It just came
blurting out.

Stewart shook his head. "Nah. They
wouldn't want me. I'm not a good
swimmer."

"You could practice," I told him. "I couldn't swim well either, at first. I only went because of my asthma."

"Yeah?" he asked.

At the pool that afternoon, I spoke to Coach. "You know that boy, Stewart Rider? I think he wants to join the swim team."

"That loser from the gas station?" he said. "We don't need him."

But the next morning Coach called. "Rachel, does that friend of yours still want to swim? Tony Valetto's broken his arm ... Now we're one short for the relay. Tell him to come."

"He can't swim very well, Coach," I reminded him.

"Just send him along," said Coach, "and I'll have him swimming before you can sneeze."

After school I went by the gas station, and there was Stewart, his feet sticking out from under a car.

"Hey, Stewart. You have to come to swimming tonight! We need another person for the relay."

Stewart rolled out from under the car.

"They want me?" he asked. "But I'm too slow."

"I told the coach and he said to come. Don't worry. He'll help you. See you tonight."

Stewart did come to the pool. Coach took one look and said, "You. In the water. Down at the shallow end. And do what I say."

Stewart learned fast, and soon he was swimming well.

Chapter 5

The Drain

The meet was only a week away when two things happened: it began to rain and I caught a cold. Mom drove Prince and me to the pool one wet afternoon. I didn't tell her my chest felt really tight. But I couldn't fool Coach.

"No swimming for you today, Rachel," he said. "Go home."

"But I'll miss the final selection," I cried.

"I'm sorry. But breathing like that, you're not going to win anyway," he said matter-of-factly.

I didn't have the energy to argue, and besides, I knew he was right. So Prince and I started for home. Prince must have sensed that I felt bad, and he kept close to me.

The rain had stopped but there were muddy puddles along the way.

We passed the empty junkyard and came to an open ditch. Usually we ran across it, but today it was full of brown, frothy water rushing along to the big underground drain.

I should have turned back, but I was too tired to take another way home.

"Come on, boy," I told Prince. "Once we cross this, we'll be home in no time."

I began to wade across the ditch, but the surging water swept my feet from under me and I fell down hard. Gasping and spluttering, I tried to stand, but the water was too strong. It was flowing fast, hurrying me toward the underground drain. I went under again.

Water went up my nose and into my mouth. I coughed and choked. I tried to grasp something with my hands but there was nothing to grip.

"Prince!" I screamed, "HELP!"

I felt something dragging at my shirt. My head went under again. I don't remember any more.

When I came to, I was lying face down on the edge of the ditch.

"Are you all right, Rachel?" It was Stewart Rider's voice.

"I ... I think so," I said. Prince was standing over me. He licked my face, wagged his tail, and then shook himself.

"Come on," said Stewart, holding out his hand to help me up. "I'll take you home. I was coming down the sidewalk when Prince nearly knocked me over. He kept barking and running back and forth as if he wanted me to follow him. And that's how I found you lying here."

"Prince, you saved my life," I said, giving him a soggy hug. "If you hadn't been here, I would have drowned."

Chapter 6

The Best Dog

I got bronchitis and had to stay in bed for three days. I missed the swim meet, but Coach came to see me. "Don't worry," he told me. "You'll be on the team next time for sure."

Stewart's team won the boys' relay and he came and thanked me. He said if it wasn't for me, he wouldn't have won anything.

The funny thing is, I didn't mind missing out. I knew Prince was the best dog in the world, and he had saved my life. Coach, Stewart, and Prince all thought I was all right.

Medals ... who needs them!